A First Thesaurus

By Harriet Wittels and Joan Greisman

A GOLDEN BOOK ❖ NEW YORK
Golden Books Publishing Company, Inc.
New York, New York 10106

For Brad, Sherry, Mark, Adam, Craig, and Amy

Cover design: James Reyman
Cover Illustration: Claude Martinot

Introduction

Riddle: What sounds like Brontosaurus, but is found on a bookshelf near the dictionaries, not at the natural history museum?

Answer: A thesaurus, of course! A thesaurus is a book that lists synonyms—words that have almost the same meaning; and antonyms—words of opposite meaning. **A First Thesaurus** will give you many accurate, interesting, and colorful new words to use, in addition to the old ones you already know. You will find this book useful, helpful, practical, handy, valuable, and beneficial. That is its aim, purpose, goal, object, and target.

Using the Thesaurus

Entry Words

The words in **A First Thesaurus** that have synonyms and antonyms are called **entry words**. They are listed in alphabetical order, and printed in dark type:

bleak dreary, dismal   cheerful
blend mix, combine, join   separate
bless praise, thank, glorify   curse

Look in the "A" section. What entry word comes just before **accident**? (Answer: **accept**.) Now look in the "B's." What entry word comes right after **brand**? Look in the "C's." Between which two entry words do you find **car**?

Guide Words

The two words at the top of every page, in dark type, are called **guide words**. They are the first and last entry words on each page, and they will "guide" you to all the entry words between them.

Here's an example: If the guide words were **change** and **chop**, you would find the entry word **chest** on that page. But you would not find the entry word **climb** on that page. Now look up the entry word **decide**. What are the two guide words at the top of the page?

Synonyms

Synonyms are words that have the same, or almost the

same, meaning. Here are two groups of synonyms:

> **embarrassed**   ashamed, humiliated, mortified
> **embrace**   grasp, hug, hold, clutch

Synonyms can usually be substituted for one another in a sentence:

> **fad**   style, fashion, craze, rage
> Blue jeans are now the fad.
> Blue jeans are now the style.
> Blue jeans are now the fashion.
> Blue jeans are now the craze.
> Blue jeans are now the rage.

But sometimes synonyms cannot be substituted for one another in a sentence. Look at this group:

> **match**   contest, game, battle
> Today we had a spelling match in our class.
> Today we had a spelling contest in our class.
> Today we had a spelling game in our class.

But you wouldn't say:
> Today we had a spelling battle in our class.

When you look up a word in this book, you may find that not all of the synonyms fit correctly in your sentence. You'll have to use common sense and good judgment in choosing the right word.

Antonyms

A word that has the opposite meaning to that of the entry

word is called an **antonym**. You will find it in red, at the end of a group of synonyms:

> **like**   enjoy, admire, appreciate   dislike
> **misty**   cloudy, foggy, smoky   clear

Here's an example:

> She doesn't like short hair, so she wears hers long.

The word "long" is the antonym of the word "short."

Now you try. Look up the entry word in dark type and find the antonyms to complete these sentences:

> Cinderella was **beautiful**, but her stepsisters were
>
> _____.
>
> It takes longer to **pack** the car than to _____ it.

Entry Words With More Than One Meaning

Some entry words, like **tag**, have more than one meaning. Tag could mean follow, shadow, trail, pursue, or tail. But tag could also mean label, name, or brand. That's why tag has two numbers for the two groups of synonyms. Here's another example:

> **tape**   1. wrap, bind, tie
> **tape**   2. record

In this book, the entry word **run** has five numbers for its five different meanings. Look up the entry word **run**, and in the following sentences, find the number of the correct group of synonyms.

The computer can only <u>run</u> on electricity. (Answer: 3.)
Will Tom <u>run</u> for class president this term? (?)
Susan had to <u>run</u> to catch the bus. (?)
Let the water <u>run</u> until it's cold. (?)
Our principal knows how to <u>run</u> our school. (?)

Entry Words That Are Spelled the Same
Some entry words are spelled the same, but we say them differently and they have completely different meanings. That's why these words have different numbers in front of them. Look at the two entry words below and how they are used.

1. minute   instant, moment
2. minute   tiny, small, miniature   giant
   Billy's dog runs to him the <u>minute</u> he whistles. (**1.**)
   You must use a microscope to see those <u>minute</u>
     germs. (**2.**)

Now see if you can complete the sentences below with the correct entry word and its number.

1. close   shut, fasten, lock   open
2. close   near, approaching   far
   School children love the month of June, because
     summer vacation is _____.
   Please _____ the door behind you.

That's how **A First Thesaurus** works. It's easy and fun. Use it often. Make it a habit and you'll find that it will help to improve your reading, your writing, and your speech.

A

abandon   desert, forsake, leave

ability   skill, talent, know-how   inability

abnormal   odd, unnatural, irregular   normal

about   1. almost, nearly, approximately, around

about   2. concerning, of

abrupt   sudden, unexpected   expected

absent   away, truant   present

absorb   take in, soak up, sponge

absurd   unbelievable, ridiculous, ludicrous   sensible

abuse   mistreat, damage

accept   adopt, believe, approve, consent to   deny

accident   mishap, fluke

accomplish   complete, do, carry out, finish, achieve

account   story, reason, description, statement

accumulate   collect, assemble, gather, compile,
  store up

accurate   correct, right, perfect   inaccurate, wrong

accuse   blame, charge

actor

ache   pain, throb, hurt

achieve   accomplish, fulfill

act   perform, behave

active   lively, peppy, spirited, energetic   inactive, lazy

actor   performer, entertainer

actual   real, true, genuine, authentic

add   put together, join   subtract

adequate   enough, sufficient, satisfactory   insufficient

admire   like, respect, appreciate

admit   1. confess, acknowledge   deny

admit   2. allow to enter, receive

adore   love, worship, idolize, cherish, revere   hate

adult   grown-up, mature   immature, juvenile

advance   proceed, progress, further   recede

advertise   announce, publicize, promote

advise   suggest, recommend, direct, counsel

affair   1. happening, occasion, occurrence, event, party, festivity

affair   2. business, concern, interest

affection   liking, fondness   dislike

afraid   frightened, scared, alarmed   unafraid, fearless

again   once more, another time

agony   suffering, pain, distress, torture

agree   consent to, comply with, approve of   disagree, differ with

agreement   pact, contract, treaty, bargain, deal, understanding

aid   help, assist, support, serve   hinder

aim   purpose, goal, object, target

alarm   scare, frighten, startle, shock, unnerve   calm, soothe

alert   wide-awake, watchful, ready   dull

alibi   excuse, story

allow   permit, let   forbid, deny

allowance   allotment, grant, budget

almost   about, nearly, approximately, practically

alone   solitary, isolated, sole

also   too, in addition, besides, as well

always   forever, for good, for keeps   never

amend   change, correct, improve

among   surrounded by, amid, in with

amount   sum, quantity

amusing   funny, entertaining, delightful, comical, humorous   boring, dull

anchor   1. fasten, fix, secure, attach

anchor   2. ship hook

anchor (2)

11

ancient old, aged, antique modern, new

angry furious, enraged, annoyed, cross

animal beast, creature

announce state, broadcast, proclaim, make known

annoy bother, disturb, tease, irritate, anger, pester, provoke

answer reply, response question

apparel clothing, dress, garments, attire

appear 1. seem, look

appear 2. arrive, approach, enter

appliance tool, device, instrument, implement, utensil, gadget

appoint choose, name, assign, nominate

appreciate enjoy, value, respect, admire

appropriate suitable, fitting, proper inappropriate, unsuitable

approximately nearly, closely, roughly, about exactly

area region, district, section, location, territory, zone

argue disagree, quarrel, squabble, bicker agree

arid dry, waterless, parched wet

arm equip, fortify, empower disarm

army troops, forces, military

aroma odor, fragrance, scent

arrange   organize, put in order, classify, sort

arrest   stop, seize, apprehend, capture

arrive   come, reach, get to, show up   go

article   1. story, essay, report

article   2. item, thing, object

ashamed   embarrassed, humiliated, mortified   proud

ask   request, question, inquire   answer

assassinate   kill, murder

assault   attack, offense, onslaught

assemble   1. meet, gather together, congregate   scatter

assemble   2. put together, set up, construct, build   demolish, take apart

assignment   task, chore, job, duty

assist   help, aid, support, lend a hand   hinder

assorted   various, several, different, mixed

astonishing   surprising, astounding, amazing

athletic   sporting, gymnastic

attach   fasten, join, connect, add   detach

attack   charge, bombard, ambush, storm, invade, raid

attempt   try, undertake, endeavor, strive

attend   go to, be present

attention   care, consideration, concern, thoughtfulness

attract   pull, interest, draw, lure   repel

attractive   lovely, pleasing, pretty, handsome
  unattractive, plain

author   writer

autograph   signature

average   ordinary, usual, common   unusual

award   prize, reward

awful   terrible, horrible, dreadful, atrocious   pleasant

awkward   clumsy, ungraceful, cumbersome, ungainly
  graceful

award

B

baby   infant, toddler

bad   evil, naughty   good

balance   equalize, stabilize, steady

bald   hairless, bare   hairy

band   orchestra

bandit   robber, thief, gangster, highwayman, outlaw

bar   1. shut out, ban, block, exclude   allow

bar   2. saloon, tavern

bald

14

bare   uncovered, naked   covered

barely   scarcely, hardly

barter   trade, exchange, swap

bashful   shy, timid, modest, coy   bold

basic   fundamental, essential

bat   strike, hit, club

battle   fight, feud, war, struggle, combat, conflict

bawl   cry, weep

beach   shore, coast, seaside

beam   shine, glow

beast   animal, creature

beat   1. strike, hit, thrash, pound, pummel

beat   2. outdo, defeat, surpass, trounce

beautiful   attractive, lovely, pretty, handsome   ugly

before   earlier, previously, prior, formerly   after

beg   plead, implore

begin   start, commence, launch   end, conclude

behind   after, later than   ahead

believe   1. think, suppose, imagine, consider

believe   2. accept, trust   doubt

belly   stomach, abdomen

beneath   under, below   above

beneficial   helpful, useful, advantageous   harmful

bet wager, gamble

between among, betwixt

beyond farther, past

big 1. large, huge, tremendous, enormous, immense
small

big 2. important, great, grand, considerable
unimportant

birth beginning, origin, infancy death, end

bitter distasteful, unpleasant pleasant, sweet

blade

blade sword, knife

blame accuse, charge, indict

blank empty, vacant filled

blast explosion, blowout

bleak dreary, dismal cheerful

blend mix, combine, join separate

bless praise, thank, glorify curse

blind sightless

blizzard snowstorm

block obstruct, hinder, check, restrain permit

blockade barrier, obstruction, barricade

bluff deceive, trick, delude

board mount, get on, embark dismount, get off

boisterous noisy, rowdy, shrill quiet

16

bold 1. brave, courageous, fearless, gallant, heroic cowardly

bold 2. arrogant, brazen, defiant, insolent timid

bolt 1. run, flee, break away

bolt 2. lock, fastener

boring dull, uninteresting interesting

boss 1. supervise, oversee, direct

boss 2. manager, foreman, employer

bother annoy, pester, disturb, irritate, harass, provoke

bottom base, foundation, lowest part top

bound enclosed, surrounded

boundary limit, border

box 1. fight, hit

box 2. crate, container

box (2)

brace support, prop

brag boast, crow, gloat

brake stop, slow down, decelerate, curb accelerate

branch shoot, bough, limb

brand kind, sort, type

brave bold, courageous, fearless, gallant, heroic cowardly

brawl riot, racket, fracas

branch

break 1. fracture, crack, crush, split, smash, shatter mend, fix

break 2. interruption, interval, intermission, pause, recess, rest

brief short, concise, terse long

bright 1. cheerful, sunny, shiny, vivid, sparkling, gleaming, glowing dull, dim

bright 2. smart, alert, intelligent dull

brilliant intelligent, wise stupid

bring carry, take, transport, deliver

broad wide, expansive narrow

bruise wound, injure, hurt

buddy friend, pal, companion, chum, partner

build make, create, construct, establish, form demolish

bulky broad, thick, lumpy narrow

bulletin message, newsletter

bumpy uneven, rocky, coarse smooth

bundle parcel, package

burglar thief, robber, housebreaker

burning

burning hot, fiery, sizzling, blazing, flaming

bury conceal, cover uncover

business work, occupation, profession, job

busy active, occupied, engaged idle

button fasten, clasp, close unbutton, open

buy purchase, shop sell

18

by   near, beside, at

C

cable   telegraph, wire
cafeteria   restaurant, snack bar, cafe
calculate   compute, count, figure, estimate
call   1. shout, yell
call   2. telephone
calm   quiet, still, peaceful, serene, tranquil
camouflage   disguise
campaign   crusade, movement, cause, drive
can   container, tin, receptacle
cancel   erase, wipe out, repeal
candidate   applicant, nominee
cap   top, cover, crown
capture   seize, arrest, catch, trap, apprehend   free, release
car   automobile, vehicle
care   1. thought, worry, attention, concern   neglect
care   2. protection, supervision, custody
careful   cautious, watchful   careless

can

19

carpet

chair

careless   sloppy, reckless, thoughtless   careful
carnival   fair, festival
carpet   rug, mat
carry   hold, transport, tote
carve   cut, slice
catalog   list, classify, group, sort
catastrophe   tragedy, disaster, calamity
catch   capture, seize, trap   release, free
cautious   careful, watchful, thoughtful   careless
cease   stop, end, halt, quit, conclude, discontinue
   continue
celebrate   1. proclaim, observe, commemorate
celebrate   2. rejoice
cemetery   graveyard
center   middle, heart, hub, core, nucleus
certain   sure, positive, definite   unsure
chair   seat, bench
challenge   dare, defy, confront
champion   winner, victor, best
chance   1. opportunity, occasion
chance   2. possibility, likelihood, prospect
chance   3. fate, luck
change   alter, modify, vary, switch   maintain
chapter   section, part, division

20

character 1. nature, temperament, makeup, disposition

character 2. role, part

charming appealing, pleasing, delightful unpleasant

chase 1. follow, run after, pursue

chase 2. drive away, repulse, reject

chat talk, gossip, discuss, converse

cheap inexpensive, low-priced expensive

cheat trick, deceive, swindle, defraud, dupe, bamboozle, mislead

check 1. restrain, curb, stop, control

check 2. prove, mark, verify

cheerful happy, glad, joyful, jolly, gay, merry sad, downcast

chest box, locker, safe

child youngster, kid adult

chilly cool, brisk, nippy warm

chisel sculpture, carve

choke strangle, suffocate, smother

choose pick, select, elect, opt

chop cut, cleave, sever, hack

chore task, job, work, assignment

chubby plump, fat, stout, stocky skinny

chubby

chuckle giggle, laugh, titter

chum friend, pal, companion, partner

city metropolis, municipality

clamor racket, ruckus, din, uproar, commotion
stillness, quiet

clean spotless, spick-and-span dirty

clear 1. remove, eliminate, rid

clear 2. bright, shining, vivid muddy, dull

clever smart, alert, bright, skillful, wise, sharp,
intelligent, quick-witted dull

client customer, patron

climate weather

climb mount, rise, ascend descend

clip 1. cut, shear, crop, snip

clip 2. fasten, attach

1. close 1. shut, fasten, lock open

close 2. end, finish, complete, conclude, stop start

2. close near, approaching far

cloudy dark, overcast, dismal clear

club 1. group, association, clique

club 2. bat, stick

club 3. strike, hit, knock

clue sign, hint, evidence, lead

club (2)

22

clumsy awkward, ungraceful, ungainly, gawky
graceful

coach train, tutor, teach

coarse 1. rough, uneven, bumpy, rocky, ragged
smooth

coarse 2. crude, vulgar, common refined

code laws, rules

cold chilly, frosty hot

collapse fall, topple

collect gather, accumulate, assemble scatter

colossal huge, gigantic, vast, immense, enormous,
mammoth tiny

combine join, unite, mix, blend, merge separate

comedian comic, funnyman

comfortable satisfied, contented, cozy, snug
uncomfortable

comical amusing, entertaining, funny, humorous,
witty

command order, direct, instruct

committee group, council, delegation

common 1. regular, ordinary, usual, familiar, everyday unusual, odd

common 2. coarse, crude, vulgar refined

commotion racket, ruckus, disturbance, tumult, confusion, fuss, excitement, clamor, hubbub, to-do
order, calmness

communicate inform, tell, enlighten

community district, area, town

companion friend, pal, chum, partner

company 1. business, firm, enterprise

company 2. guests, visitors

compare match, liken, contrast

complete 1. end, finish, conclude, wind up start

complete 2. whole, entire incomplete

complicated hard, involved, difficult, complex
simple

compliment praise, commend, flatter

conceal hide, cover, mask, camouflage disclose,
reveal

conceited vain, boastful, cocky, egotistical modest

concern 1. interest, care, worry

concern 2. business, company, firm

concert musical performance, recital

conclude end, finish, complete, close, stop open,
begin

condition circumstance, situation, state

1. conduct manage, direct, lead, guide

2. conduct behavior, manner

confident certain, sure, convinced, self-reliant
doubtful

confuse   complicate, bewilder, dumfound, muddle, baffle, perplex, puzzle   clarify

congratulate   compliment, commend, praise

connect   join, unite, combine, link, attach   separate, disconnect

conquer   overcome, overwhelm, overtake, overthrow, defeat, crush

consent   permission, approval, acceptance, agreement   refusal

conserve   keep, save, preserve   waste

consider   think, study, ponder, contemplate, imagine

considerate   thoughtful, kind, sympathetic, tactful   inconsiderate, unkind

console   comfort, reassure, soothe

constantly   continually, always

construct   make, manufacture, build, form, create, assemble   demolish

consume   eat, devour

contain   hold, include, consist of, comprise

contented   satisfied, pleased   discontented, dissatisfied

contest   game, tournament, competition

continue   persist, go on, keep on   discontinue, stop

control   restrain, check, curb

convenient   easy, handy, suitable   inconvenient

conversation talk, chat, discussion

convert change, transform

convict condemn, sentence clear, acquit

convince persuade

cool 1. chilly warm

cool 2. calm, unexcited excited

cooperate support, help, work together, collaborate hinder

copy imitate, duplicate, echo, repeat, reproduce

correct 1. right, true, accurate, proper, exact, appropriate incorrect, wrong

correct 2. improve, remedy

correspond write, communicate with

corridor hallway, passageway, aisle

counterfeit fake, imitation, copied real

country nation, land

courageous brave, bold, fearless, gallant, heroic cowardly

course line, track, direction

courteous polite, respectful, civil, gracious rude

cover 1. hide, conceal, protect, shelter uncover

cover 2. include, contain, consist of, comprise

cowardly timid, weak brave

coy timid, shy, modest, bashful bold

crack break, split, fracture

crammed stuffed, full, heaping, overflowing, loaded, packed, crowded, jammed

cranky cross, annoyed, irritable, grouchy, disagreeable
  pleasant

crazy insane, mad, daft sane

create make, invent, originate, shape, form, manufac-ture, produce, design, establish

crew team, gang, staff, force

crime wrongdoing, sin, vice, evil

crook criminal, gangster, lawbreaker

cross cranky, annoyed, irritable, grouchy, disagree-able pleasant

crowd mob, throng, horde

cruel mean, unkind, heartless, brutal, ruthless kind

crush press, squeeze, compress, squash

cry weep, wail, sob, bawl

cuddle snuggle, nestle

cure heal, remedy

curious inquisitive, nosy, prying, snoopy
  uninterested

current 1. up-to-date, present, prevalent, new
  old-fashioned

current 2. flow, stream

curse swear, condemn

cry

27

curve bend, wind, twist, turn

custom way, manner, tradition, habit, practice

customer client, buyer, patron

cut 1. snip, clip, slit, slash, saw, sever

cut 2. shorten, reduce, abbreviate, condense, abridge increase

cute attractive, bright, pretty unattractive

D

dainty delicate, fine, small gross

damage harm, hurt, impair, spoil mend, fix

damp moist, wet dry

dangerous unsafe, risky, hazardous safe

daring brave, bold, courageous, fearless, heroic afraid, timid

dark dim, gloomy, dismal, somber, dreary bright

dart dash, rush, hurry, scurry dawdle

dash dart, rush, hurry, scurry dawdle

data facts, information

date appointment, engagement

dawdle idle, loiter, linger, delay, tarry hurry

dawn daybreak, sunrise dusk

dazzling brilliant, shiny, glowing, glistening, blinding dull

dead lifeless, deceased, gone alive

deal agreement, understanding, bargain, transaction

debate argue, dispute

deceive cheat, trick, swindle, defraud, dupe, bamboozle, mislead

decent proper, correct, suitable improper

decide settle, determine, resolve, judge

declare say, state, exclaim, announce

decorate beautify, trim, adorn

decorate

decrease reduce, lessen, diminish, cut, shorten increase

deduct subtract, remove, withdraw add

defeat overcome, triumph, outdo, surpass

defend protect, safeguard, shield, support attack

define explain, describe, clarify

definite clear, precise, clear-cut, exact unclear

deform spoil, disfigure, mar

delay postpone, put off, detain, stall

deliberately purposely, intentionally, knowingly accidentally

delicate   mild, fine, dainty, fragile   gross

delicious   luscious, tasty, appetizing   tasteless

delighted   happy, jubilant, overjoyed, elated
unhappy

delightful   pleasant, lovely, charming, appealing,
pleasing   unpleasant

deliver   hand over, transfer

demand   ask, request

demolish   wreck, destroy, dismantle   restore

demon   devil, fiend, monster, ogre

demonstrate   show, display, present, exhibit, illustrate

depart

depart   leave, exit   arrive

dependable   trustworthy, reliable   undependable

deposit   place, put, leave   withdraw

depressed   sad, dejected, discouraged, downhearted,
blue   happy

deprived   wanting, lacking, needing, missing, without

describe   define, portray, depict, characterize

desert   leave, forsake, abandon

deserve   earn, merit

design   draw, plan, sketch

desire   wish, want, long for

despise   hate, loathe, detest   love

destination   goal, end, objective

destroy   spoil, ruin, wreck   restore

detach   separate, unfasten, disconnect   attach

detest   despise, hate, loathe   love

detour   by-pass

detour

develop   grow, mature, progress, advance, flourish

devil   demon, fiend, ogre, monster

devotion   1. love, affection, fondness

devotion   2. loyalty, dedication

devour   eat, consume

diagram   drawing, sketch, design

diary   account, record

die   pass away, perish, expire   live

diary

different   unlike, distinct   same

difficult   hard, complicated, troublesome   easy

dig   scoop, excavate

dignified   noble, majestic, grand, distinguished
undignified

dim   dull, dark, faint, weak, indistinct   bright

dimension   measurement, size, proportions

dingy   dirty, dull, dark   bright

direct   1. show, point out, guide, lead, steer, escort

direct   2. manage, control, conduct, lead, head, guide,
command

dig

31

dirty

dirty soiled, filthy clean

disadvantage drawback, handicap advantage

disagree differ, quarrel, dispute, argue, oppose agree

disappear vanish, fade away appear

disaster tragedy, calamity, misfortune, catastrophe

discard throw away, reject, scrap keep

discharge dismiss, release, unload, dump

discipline punish, correct, chastise

discouraged depressed, dejected, downhearted encouraged

discover find, uncover, reveal, unearth

discuss talk over

disease sickness, illness, ailment, malady

disgrace shame, embarrassment

disguise conceal, mask, camouflage reveal

disgusted sickened, offended, nauseated, revolted

dishonest untruthful, deceitful, crooked, untrustworthy honest

dismal dark, gloomy, dreary, bleak, depressing bright

dismiss discharge, expel, release

display show, present, exhibit, demonstrate

dispute argue, quarrel, fight agree

32

distinct   plain, clear, obvious, exact, definite, clear-cut
unclear

distinguished   famous, honored, outstanding, celebrated, dignified

distribute   dispense, allot, disperse   collect

district   area, region, section, neighborhood, zone

disturb   upset, annoy, bother

divide   separate, split   unite

divorce   separate, split   marry

dizzy   unsteady, confused, spinning   steady

dock   anchor, moor

dock

doctor   physician, medic

document   certificate, statement

dodge   duck, avoid, evade

donate   contribute, give, present, grant

done   complete, finished, ended, concluded
unfinished

donkey   burro, ass

dose   portion, amount, quantity

doubt   question, mistrust, suspect   believe, trust

downfall   defeat, failure, ruin

donkey

downpour   rainstorm, cloudburst, flood

drab   dull, lifeless, flat, unattractive   bright,
attractive

draft 1. wind, air current

draft 2. enlistment, enrollment, call-up, recruitment, induction

drag pull, tug, draw, haul, tow

drain empty, extract, draw off, remove   fill

dramatize produce, present, stage

draw 1. sketch, portray, picture

draw 2. attract, lure   repel

dreadful awful, terrible, horrible, vile, ghastly, wretched   wonderful

dream imagine, fantasize

dreary gloomy, dull, dismal, dim, dark   bright

drench soak, wet, flood, saturate

dress clothe, outfit, attire

drill practice, teach, train, exercise

drive steer, handle, operate

drizzle rain, shower, sprinkle

droop sag, drag, hang, dangle

drop end, cease, stop, let go, give up   start, continue

drown sink, submerge, immerse

drowsy sleepy, dreamy   alert

drug medicine, narcotic

drunk intoxicated, inebriated, tipsy   sober

dry arid, parched   wet

duck dodge, avoid, evade

dress

34

dull 1. dim, dark, faint, weak, indistinct bright

dull 2. stupid, slow, dim-witted, dumb smart

dull 3. boring, uninteresting, monotonous interesting

dumb 1. stupid, dull, dim-witted smart

dumb 2. speechless, mute, silent

dummy 1. imitation, copy, model

dummy 2. dope, dolt, dunce, fool

dump empty, unload, discard, scrap, throw away load

dunce dummy, dope, dolt, fool

duplicate copy, repeat, reproduce, double

dusk sunset, sundown, evening, nightfall dawn

duty task, job, chore, work, assignment, obligation, responsibility

dye color, stain, tint

dynamic active, energetic, forceful, intense weak

E

eager anxious, enthusiastic

earn deserve, merit, gain

earth (2)

earth 1. soil, dirt, ground

earth 2. world, globe

easy simple, plain, uncomplicated hard

eat dine, consume

echo reflect, resound, reverberate

eclipse blackout, shadow

edge border, frame, rim

edit correct, check, rewrite, revise, amend

educate teach, train, tutor, instruct, enlighten

eerie weird, spooky, strange, ghostly

effort try, attempt, undertaking, endeavor

elastic flexible, springy, stretchable inflexible

elder older, senior younger

elect pick, select, choose

elegant refined, tasteful, polished common, vulgar

elementary basic, beginning, introductory, fundamental, primary advanced

elevate lift, raise, boost, hoist lower

eligible qualified, fit, suitable ineligible

eliminate discard, remove, throw out, reject, exclude
include

else other, different

embarrassed ashamed, humiliated, mortified

embrace grasp, hug, hold, clutch

emergency crisis, pinch

emotion feeling, sentiment

emphasize stress, accent, highlight

employ hire, sign up, engage fire

empty blank, vacant, hollow, barren full

enclosed surrounded, fenced, contained, restricted, encircled open

encourage urge, nudge, prod, support, inspire discourage

end finish, stop, cease, complete, conclude, terminate, discontinue, quit begin

endless constant, continuous, nonstop, infinite

enemy foe, opponent, opposition friend

energy strength, force, power, might, vitality, pep, vigor

engrave print, inscribe, stamp, carve

enjoy like, admire, relish dislike

enlarge expand, inflate, increase, amplify, magnify reduce, shrink

enlist enroll, register, sign up, join

enormous huge, giant, immense, vast, gigantic, colossal tiny

enough plenty, sufficient, ample, adequate insufficient

enraged angry, mad, furious, provoked

enroll enlist, register, join, sign up

entertaining interesting, amusing, fascinating, absorbing, delightful boring, dull

enthusiastic eager, interested indifferent

entire whole, full, complete, total partial

envious jealous

environment neighborhood, surroundings

equal tie, match, parallel

equip provide, furnish, supply, outfit

erase rub out, cancel

erect build, construct

errand task, job, assignment, chore

escape flee, get away

escort accompany, chaperone

essay composition, article, paper

essential important, needed, necessary, vital
  unimportant

establish create, set up, organize, form

estimate figure, judge, guess, compute, calculate

etiquette manners, rules of conduct, amenities

evaporate fade away, disappear, vanish

even 1. level, flat, smooth uneven

even 2. same, equal, identical different

evening sunset, sundown, dusk, nightfall morning

event incident, happening, experience, occurrence

eventually finally, in time, ultimately

evict expel, oust, turn out

evidence   facts, proof, signs, clues

evil   bad, sinful, wicked   good

exactly   precisely

exaggerate   magnify, stretch, overstate   minimize

examine   1. inspect, study, observe

examine   2. test, quiz, question

example   sample, model, specimen

excellent   very good, fine, splendid, superb   inferior

except   excluding, besides, barring   including

exceptional   notable, outstanding, unusual, extraordinary, remarkable   ordinary

exchange   trade, change, substitute, switch, swap

excited   enthusiastic, eager, interested   indifferent

excursion   trip, journey, tour, outing

1. excuse   reason, alibi

2. excuse   pardon, forgive, absolve   blame

executive   administrator, manager, director, officer

exercise   practice, drill, train, prepare, condition

exercise

exhausted   tired, weary, fatigued   energetic

exhibit   show, display, present, demonstrate

exile   banish, expel, deport

exit   depart, go out, leave   enter

expand   spread, grow, enlarge, increase, broaden   contract, reduce

expect   look for, await, anticipate

expedition   journey, trip, pilgrimage

expel   remove, discharge, dismiss, oust   admit

expensive   costly, high-priced, dear   cheap

experience   event, incident, happening, occurrence

experiment   try, test

expired   ended, ceased, discontinued

explain   clarify, describe, simplify

explode   burst, blow up

explore   search, research, investigate, probe

express   1. fast, quick, speedy, rapid, swift   slow

express   2. present, tell, describe

exquisite   beautiful, gorgeous, stunning, dazzling
ugly

extend   increase, enlarge, stretch, lengthen, expand,
broaden   reduce, decrease

exterminate   destroy, get rid of, eliminate, kill,
wipe out

extinct   dead, gone, obsolete

extinguish   put out, smother, crush

extra   additional, more, spare, surplus

extraordinary   special, unusual, remarkable, exceptional, noteworthy, memorable   ordinary

extreme   exaggerated, overdone, extravagant
moderate

F

fable   story, fairy tale, legend, myth

fabric   cloth, material

fabulous   wonderful, marvelous, splendid, superb, spectacular, remarkable

face   meet, confront, encounter

fact   detail, item, point

factory   plant

fad   style, fashion, craze, rage

fade   dim, lose color, weaken

fail   flop, flunk, be unsuccessful   succeed

faint   1. weak, dim, faded, pale, dull, hazy   strong, bright

faint   2. black out, swoon, weaken

fair   1. right, correct, just, honest, impartial   unfair, unjust

fair   2. sunny, clear, pleasant, bright   cloudy

fair   3. average, mediocre

fair   4. light, pale   dark

fair   5. festival, bazaar

fabric

fall (1)

fairy   elf, pixie, sprite

faith   1. trust, hope, belief, confidence

faith   2. religion, teaching

fake   imitation, false, counterfeit   real

fall   1. drop, descend, tumble, topple, plunge, collapse   rise

fall   2. autumn

false   1. wrong, incorrect, untrue   true

false   2. fake, counterfeit   real

familiar   popular, well-known, common   strange

family   group, kin, relatives, folks

famous   popular, well-known, celebrated, renowned

fan   admirer, follower

fancy   elaborate, frilly, flowery, fussy, ornate   simple, plain

fantastic   incredible, unusual, extraordinary, exceptional, remarkable, wonderful, marvelous   ordinary

far   distant, remote, removed   near

fare   charge, toll, fee

farm   grow, raise, harvest, cultivate

fascinating   interesting, absorbing, exciting, thrilling, captivating   boring

fashion   1. make, form, shape, create, mold

fashion   2. style, mode, vogue

fast   rapid, swift, speedy, quick   slow

farm

fasten   secure, tie, bind, attach, close, seal   untie, open

fat   heavy, stout, plump, chubby   thin

faucet   spigot, tap

fault   mistake, error

favor   good deed, kindness, service

favorite   best, choice, prized, pet

fear   fright, dread, alarm, panic, terror

fearless   brave, daring, bold, courageous, heroic   afraid

feast   banquet, treat

fee   charge, fare, toll, dues

feeble   weak, frail   strong

feed   nourish, supply, nurture

feel   touch, handle, finger

female   feminine, womanly   male

fence   1. enclosure, wall, barrier

fence   2. fight, duel, joust

ferocious   fierce, savage, vicious, brutal, cruel, wild, ruthless   tame

fertile   fruitful, rich, productive   barren

feud   fight, disagree, argue, dispute, quarrel, battle

fib   lie, untruth, falsehood

field   land, tract, plot

fiend   devil, demon, monster, ogre

fierce ferocious, violent, raging, savage, wild, vicious gentle

fiery hot, burning, flaming

fight dispute, feud, battle, struggle

figure shape, form, build, physique

file 1. sort, classify, group, categorize

file 2. grind, smooth, sand, sharpen

fill load, pack, stuff, supply empty

filter strain, screen, sift, separate

filthy dirty, grimy, polluted clean

final last, closing, concluding beginning

finale end, conclusion, finish opening

find discover, detect, learn, uncover, disclose lose

fine 1. good, excellent, splendid

fine 2. delicate, dainty rough

fine 3. penalize, charge, tax

finish end, conclude, complete, close, stop start

fire 1. blaze, flame

fire 2. dismiss, discharge, lay off hire

fire 3. shoot, discharge, blast

firm 1. hard, solid, rigid, inflexible, immovable flexible

firm 2. company, business, enterprise

fit 1. healthy, strong, well unfit

fit 2. attack, seizure, spell, convulsion

fix   repair, mend, adjust, regulate   break
flag   pennant, banner, standard
flame   fire, blaze
flat   smooth, even, level   uneven
flatter   praise, compliment
flee   run away, bolt, escape
flexible   elastic, springy, stretchable, pliable   rigid, inflexible
flimsy   weak, fragile   strong, sturdy
fling   toss, hurl, pitch, throw
flood   overfill, drench, overflow
floor   1. ground, pavement
floor   2. level, story
flower   blossom, bloom, develop, flourish
fluid   liquid, flowing, watery   solid
fly   soar, glide
foe   enemy, opponent   friend
foggy   cloudy, dim, smoky, misty   clear
fold   bend, double over, crease   unfold
follow   1. chase, trail, track, pursue
follow   2. obey, use, practice
fondness   liking, love, affection
foolish   silly, stupid, dumb, ridiculous, senseless
forbid   prohibit, bar, ban, prevent   allow

flag

fling

45

force 1. compel, make, drive, pressure, push

force 2. power, strength, energy

forecast prediction, prophecy

forgive pardon, excuse, absolve blame

forlorn sad, hopeless, melancholy, unhappy, downcast, despondent cheerful

form make, develop, shape, fashion, create, construct,
mold

fortunate lucky unlucky

forward onward, ahead backward

foundation 1. base, ground

foundation 2. establishment, organization, institution

fraction part, portion, segment

fracture break, crack, shatter, smash, split, rupture
heal

frail weak, slight, delicate, fragile strong

frame

frame border, edge, trim

frantic excited, hysterical, upset, frenzied calm

freak unusual, queer, grotesque, bizarre

free 1. release, clear, dismiss, discharge, liberate,
acquit, emancipate restrain

free 2. complimentary, gratis

frequently often, regularly, repeatedly seldom

friend companion, buddy, pal enemy

frighten   scare, alarm, terrify

frosting   icing, topping

frosty   icy, cold   hot

frown   pout, scowl   smile

full   packed, heaping, overflowing, loaded, stuffed, crowded, jammed, crammed   empty

fun   pleasure, entertainment, enjoyment

funny   amusing, entertaining, humorous, comical, laughable   sad

fur   pelt, hide, skin

furious   angry, annoyed, enraged, mad, infuriated   calm

furnish   supply, provide, equip, outfit

fuse   unite, join, combine, weld   separate

fuss   commotion, uproar, racket, riot, to-do, excitement

G

gadget   contraption, tool, device, appliance

gallant   brave, bold, courageous, fearless, heroic   cowardly

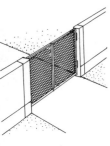

gate

gem

gamble   bet, wager, risk

gang   group, crew, ring, crowd, mob, band

gap   opening, hole, space

garbage   rubbish, trash, waste, junk, refuse

garden   plant, grow, raise, cultivate

gash   cut, wound, laceration

gate   fence, barrier

gather   collect, assemble, accumulate, amass, compile
scatter

gay   1. happy, lively, jolly, cheerful, jovial, vivacious
glum

gay   2. colorful, bright, vivid   dull

gaze   stare, gape, gawk

gem   jewel, precious stone, treasure

general   officer, commander

generous   giving, unselfish, kind, bighearted, liberal
selfish, stingy

gentle   soft, mild, tender, soothing   harsh, rough

genuine   real, true, pure, authentic   fake

ghost   spirit, phantom, spook

giant   colossal, huge, gigantic, vast, immense, enormous, mammoth   tiny

gift   1. present, offering

gift   2. talent, ability, forte

48

gigantic   colossal, huge, giant, vast, immense, enormous, mammoth   tiny

giggle   laugh, chuckle, snicker

give   present, hand over, provide, supply   take

glacier   iceberg

glad   happy, pleased, cheerful, delighted, joyful, satisfied   unhappy

glamorous   beautiful, attractive, stunning, gorgeous, dazzling   unattractive

glance   look, glimpse

glare   stare, scowl

glaring   bright, shining, glowing, flashing, dazzling, blinding   dim

gleaming   bright, shining, glowing, beaming, sparkling   dim

glide   move easily, slide, skim, coast

globe   sphere, earth, world, universe

gloomy   dark, dismal, dim, dreary, depressing, glum, bleak   cheerful

glorious   great, grand, magnificent, splendid, superb, majestic, wonderful, divine, sensational, marvelous

glowing   bright, shining, gleaming, beaming, sparkling   dim

glue   paste, cement, stick together

glue

glum   sad, gloomy, depressed, moody   cheerful

goal   aim, object, target, purpose

gobble gulp, eat fast, devour

good fine, nice, proper, right, appropriate, decent bad

gorgeous beautiful, stunning, glorious, dazzling, ravishing ugly

govern rule, control, regulate, command, manage, head, lead, supervise, direct, run

grab snatch, seize, grasp, clutch

gracious polite, pleasant, kindly, courteous, cordial, friendly rude, unkind

grade 1. mark, score

grade 2. class, division, group, category

graduate pass, succeed, advance

grand great, stately, majestic, magnificent, glorious, splendid

grant 1. give, donate, contribute, present, award

grant 2. let, allow, permit deny

grasp grab, snatch, seize, clutch, grip, hold release

grateful thankful, appreciative ungrateful

grave burial place, plot

grease oil, fat, lubrication

great grand, magnificent, glorious, splendid, superb, majestic, wonderful, sensational

grimy dirty, filthy, soiled clean

grin smile, smirk

grind   crush, mash, crumble, squash, pulverize

grip   grasp, hold, seize, clutch

gross   crude, coarse, vulgar, unrefined   refined

grotesque   deformed, monstrous, disfigured, ugly, bizarre

grouchy   annoyed, cranky, cross, irritable, disagreeable, crabby, grumpy, moody   pleasant, cheerful

group   sort, classify, arrange, organize

grow   1. develop, mature, age, progress, increase shrink

grow   2. plant, raise, cultivate

growl   snarl, grumble, complain

guarantee   promise, assure, pledge

guard   watch, protect, defend, shield, secure, patrol

guard

guess   think, believe, suppose, assume, imagine

guest   visitor, company

guide   1. show, direct, point out, lead, steer, escort

guide   2. manage, direct, control, regulate, advise, conduct

guilty   criminal, to blame, at fault   innocent

gun   weapon, firearm, pistol, revolver

gun

gymnastics   exercises, athletics, acrobatics, calisthenics

gyp   cheat, trick, deceive, swindle, defraud, dupe, bamboozle, mislead

H

hammer (2)

habit   custom, practice, pattern, routine

hall   1. corridor, passageway, vestibule

hall   2. meeting room, auditorium

halt   stop, end, conclude, quit   start

hammer   1. pound, hit, knock, bang

hammer   2. mallet

hand   give, turn over, deliver, pass, transfer

handbag   purse, pocketbook

handicap   burden, disadvantage

handle   1. feel, touch, finger, manipulate

handle   2. manage, direct, carry on, run

handsome   good-looking, attractive   ugly

handy   1. useful, nearby, ready, available, convenient   inconvenient

handy   2. skilled, expert, clever, apt, adept   clumsy, inept

happen   occur, take place

happy   glad, cheerful, contented, joyful, jolly, gay, pleased, satisfied   unhappy, sad

harbor   port, dock, pier, wharf

hard   1. firm, solid, stiff, rigid   soft

hard   2. difficult, tough, rough   easy

hardly   barely, scarcely, nearly

hardy   strong, tough, healthy, sturdy, rugged, robust   weak

harm   hurt, damage, injure, impair

harsh   cruel, severe, gruff, hard, rough, stern, tough, curt, brusque   kind

harvest   crop, produce, output, yield

hasty   1. quick, fast, swift, rapid, speedy, hurried   slow

hasty   2. rash, reckless, impulsive

hatch   produce, breed, generate

hate   detest, despise, loathe   love

haul   drag, pull, tug, tow

haunted   spooky, weird, eerie, possessed

hazardous   dangerous, unsafe, risky   safe

hazy   1. dim, cloudy, misty, overcast, foggy   clear

hazy   2. unclear, vague, fuzzy, uncertain, confused   clear

head   lead, supervise, command, direct, manage, control, conduct, run

heading   title, headline

heal cure, remedy, correct, mend, repair

heaping full, overflowing, loaded, piled, stuffed, stacked

heavy fat, stout, plump, hefty thin

hectic busy, exciting, frantic calm

help aid, assist, cooperate, support hinder

hem border, edge, rim

heroic brave, bold, courageous, fearless, gallant cowardly

hide conceal, cover, mask, camouflage reveal

hideous ugly, horrible, dreadful, awful, ghastly, wretched beautiful

high

high tall, towering, elevated low

highway road, turnpike, expressway, thruway

hilarious funny, humorous, laughable, comical

hint clue, suggestion

hire 1. employ, engage fire

hire 2. lease, rent, charter

hit strike, bat, slap, smack, slug, swat

hoist raise, lift, boost, elevate lower

hole gap, opening, cavity

hollow empty, vacant

home residence, dwelling

homely ugly, plain, unattractive attractive

honest truthful, upright, moral, ethical, honorable, sincere dishonest

hook fasten, clip, latch, clasp, snap unhook

horrible dreadful, awful, terrible, frightful, ghastly, wretched

hot 1. steaming, sweltering, sizzling, torrid cold

hot 2. spicy, sharp, peppery, tangy bland

house shelter, home, residence, dwelling

house

howl cry, yell, shout, scream, screech, roar, wail

hubbub noise, racket, commotion, disturbance, tumult, confusion, fuss, excitement, clamor, to-do stillness, calm

huddle crowd, gather, cluster, assemble

hug embrace, grasp, hold, clutch, squeeze

huge gigantic, colossal, giant, vast, immense, enormous, mammoth tiny

humble modest, plain, simple, unpretentious showy

humid moist, damp, muggy dry

humiliated embarrassed, ashamed, mortified

humorous funny, laughable, comical, witty

hunger appetite, craving, desire

hunt seek, search, look, scout

hurl toss, fling, throw, pitch

hurry rush, hasten, speed, dash, hustle

hut

hurt   harm, damage, injure, impair

husband   spouse, mate, married man

husky   sturdy, rugged, muscular, strong, athletic
slight

hut   cabin, shed, shanty, shack

hypnotize   entrance, spellbind, mesmerize

hysterical   upset, uncontrollable, frantic, overexcited,
delirious   calm

I

icing

icing   frosting, topping

idea   thought, notion, concept

identify   name, describe, label, tag

idiot   imbecile, moron, half-wit, fool, simpleton

ignore   avoid, snub, overlook

ill   sick, ailing   healthy

illegal   unlawful, criminal   legal

illustrate   picture, draw, portray

imagine   1. think, guess, suppose, believe

imagine   2. dream, fantasize, envision

56

imbecile   idiot, moron, half-wit, fool, simpleton

imitate   copy, repeat, duplicate

immediately   now, instantly, at once, promptly   later

immense   huge, giant, enormous, vast, gigantic, colossal   tiny

impatient   restless, edgy   patient

impolite   rude, disrespectful, ill-mannered, insolent   polite

important   necessary, meaningful, significant, urgent, major   unimportant

impossible   unthinkable, absurd   possible

improve   better, perfect, advance

incident   event, happening, occurrence

incinerator   furnace, burner

include   contain, cover   exclude

income   earnings, wages, pay, salary

incomplete   unfinished, partial   complete

inconsiderate   thoughtless, unkind   considerate, thoughtful

incorrect   wrong, inaccurate, faulty, mistaken   right, correct

increase   enlarge, expand, extend, inflate   decrease

incredible   unbelievable, absurd, fantastic

independent   1. acting alone, self-reliant   dependent

independent   2. neutral, impartial

indicate   show, point out, demonstrate, express, signify

indistinct   unclear, vague, cloudy, dim, hazy, blurred
clear

inexpensive   cheap, low-priced, reasonable
expensive

infect   contaminate, pollute, poison

inflate   expand, stretch   deflate

inflexible   firm, rigid, stiff   flexible

influence   move, sway, persuade

inform   tell, notify, report, instruct

information   news, facts, knowledge, data

infuriate   anger, upset, enrage, irritate, provoke
soothe

ingredient   part, element, factor, component

injure   harm, hurt, damage, impair

inn

inn   lodge, hotel, motel

innocent   blameless, without guilt   guilty

inquire   ask, question, investigate

inquisitive   curious, snooping, nosy

insane   crazy, mad, unbalanced   sane

insignia   emblems, symbols, badges

insist   urge, press, demand, push

inspect   examine, observe, study, review

inspire influence, encourage

instantly immediately, fast, promptly, quickly, rapidly, swiftly

institution organization, establishment

instruct teach, show, educate, inform, tell, advise

instrument tool, device, implement, utensil, gadget, appliance

insult offend, affront

intelligent bright, smart, alert, wise ignorant

interesting entertaining, amusing, fascinating, absorbing, captivating boring, uninteresting

interfere intrude, meddle

intermission recess, pause, break, interval

interpret explain, clarify

interrupt break in, interfere, intrude

interview question, quiz, interrogate

intrude interfere, meddle

invade raid, attack, overrun

invalid sickly, weak, unhealthy, frail healthy

invent make up, develop, originate, create, produce, discover, devise

investigate look into, explore, examine, inspect, study, probe

invite ask, call

irritable cross, cranky, annoyed, grouchy, disagreeable pleasant

irritate   1. annoy, bother, anger, infuriate, provoke
irritate   2. rub, chafe, inflame   soothe
issue   1. topic, subject, theme, question, point
issue   2. copy, edition

J

jab   poke, push, thrust
jail   lock up, imprison, incarcerate
jam   1. crowd, stuff, cram, squeeze, crush, load
jam   2. jelly, marmalade, preserve
jealous   envious
jewel   gem, stone
job   work, employment, task, assignment, duty, occupation, position

jog

jog   run, sprint
join   connect, unite, combine, link, attach   separate, detach
jolly   merry, cheerful, jovial, gay, happy, pleasant   glum
journey   expedition, trip, excursion, pilgrimage

60

joyful   jolly, merry, cheerful, jovial, gay, happy   glum

judge   referee, umpire, mediator

jumble   mix, scramble

jumbo   gigantic, colossal, huge, giant, immense, enormous   tiny

jump   spring, leap, bound

junk   rubbish, trash, scrap

just   fair, proper, moral   unjust

juvenile   young, youthful   old

jump

K

keep   save, preserve, conserve   discard

kennel   doghouse, pound

key   1. clue, hint, evidence, lead, explanation

key   2. pitch, tone, note

kid   1. tease, fool, joke, jest

kid   2. child, tot

kidnap   snatch, abduct

kill   slay, murder, slaughter, execute, assassinate

kind   1. considerate, thoughtful, sympathetic, gentle, helpful   unkind, mean

kid (2)

61

knife

kind   2. sort, type, variety

king   ruler, chief, monarch, sovereign

kit   equipment, set, furnishings, gear

knife   blade, sword

knock   hit, strike, beat, hammer, rap, bang

L

label   tag, name, title

labor   work, toil

lack   want, need, require

ladle   dipper, scoop

land   arrive, touch down, descend

lane   path, road, aisle

large   big, huge, tremendous, enormous, immense, grand, massive   small

lariat   rope, lasso

lasso   rope, lariat

last   final, end   first, beginning

latch   lock, hook, clasp, fastener

lariat

laugh   giggle, chuckle

launch   start, begin, introduce, establish

law   rule, regulation, principle, act, ordinance

lay   put, place, set

lazy   lax, idle, inactive   active

lead   guide, conduct, manage, direct, head

league   union, group, alliance

leap   jump, spring, bound

learn   1. find out, discover

learn   2. memorize

lease   rent, hire, charter

leash   strap, chain

least   fewest, smallest, minimum   most

leave   1. go, depart, exit   arrive

leave   2. quit, abandon, desert   stay

lecture   speech, talk, address

ledge   shelf, edge

ledge

legal   lawful, permitted, allowed, legitimate, author-
ized   illegal

legend   story, tale, fable, myth

lend   give, loan   borrow

lengthen   extend, stretch, prolong   shorten

less   fewer, smaller   more

lesson   assignment, exercise

Dear Mom and Dad,
Camp is great.
There are seven kids
in my bunk.
Our counselor is nice.
I learned to paddle
a canoe. Love,
Anna

letter

let   permit, allow, consent

letter   message, note, dispatch

level   flat, even, smooth   uneven

liberty   freedom, independence, emancipation

license   permission, consent, approval, authorization

lid   cover, top, cap

lie   fib, exaggerate

lift   hoist, raise, boost, elevate   lower

light   1. bright, clear   dark

light   2. weightless, airy, delicate   heavy

like   enjoy, admire, appreciate   dislike

limit   end, boundary, restriction

link   join, connect, unite, combine, attach, bridge   separate

liquid   fluid   solid

list   record, enumerate

litter   rubbish, scrap, junk, trash, garbage

little   small, tiny, minute, slight   big

live   dwell, reside

lively   active, energetic, animated, vivacious, spry, spirited, gay   dull

load   1. burden, cargo, freight

load   2. fill, stuff, pack   unload

64

loaf   idle, lounge, loiter

loan   give, lend

lobby   entrance, vestibule

location   area, place, site, spot, region

lock   fasten, close, hook, clasp, latch, shut   unlock, open

lock

logical   reasonable, sensible, rational   unreasonable

lonely   alone, friendless, isolated

look   1. see, glance, gaze, stare

look   2. seem, appear

loose   slack, limp, drooping   tight

lose   1. fail, flop, be unsuccessful   win

lose   2. misplace, mislay   find

lottery   raffle, drawing

loud   noisy, thunderous, roaring   soft

love   adore, idolize, cherish, admire   hate

lovely   attractive, pleasing, pretty, delightful, charming, appealing, beautiful   unattractive

loyal   faithful, true, devoted, trustworthy   disloyal

lucky   fortunate   unlucky

luggage   baggage, bags, suitcases, valises

luggage

luxurious   extravagant, elegant, magnificent, grand, splendid

65

M

maid

mail (2)

mad   1. crazy, insane, deranged   sane

mad   2. angry, furious, enraged, annoyed, cross, irritated

magazine   periodical, journal

magic   witchcraft, voodoo, wizardry, sorcery

magnetic   attractive, pulling, drawing

magnificent   grand, great, stately, majestic, glorious, splendid, superb, exquisite, marvelous, wonderful

magnify   enlarge, expand, exaggerate, stretch, inflate, increase, amplify   minimize

maid   servant, housekeeper, domestic

mail   1. send, dispatch

mail   2. letters, correspondence

main   chief, principal, foremost, leading

make   1. build, construct, create, manufacture, produce, form, assemble

make   2. force, cause, compel

make   3. kind, type, sort, brand

66

manage conduct, direct, lead, guide, run, operate, control, govern, supervise

manner way, style, nature, character, method

manual guidebook, handbook, directory

manufacture make, build, construct, create, produce, form, assemble

many numerous, various, several few

map

map chart

marathon race, contest

march walk, hike, parade

margin border, edge, rim

marionette puppet, doll

mark grade, rating

market store, shop, mart

marvelous wonderful, extraordinary, glorious, great, grand, magnificent, splendid, superb, divine, sensational, spectacular ordinary

mash crush, crumble, grind, pulverize

mask disguise, camouflage

marionette

masquerade disguise, pretend, pose, impersonate

master head, chief, ruler, commander

match contest, game, battle

mature full-grown, adult, developed, ripe immature

maximum most, greatest, largest minimum

maybe perhaps, possibly

meadow

meadow   pasture, field, grassland

mean   1. suggest, signify, imply

mean   2. unkind, cross, irritable, malicious   kind

mechanic   repairman, technician

medal   award, prize, honor, medallion

medicine   drug, cure, remedy

meek   shy, timid, gentle, tame, mild, modest   aggressive

meet   assemble, gather, congregate, unite

melody   tune, song

melt   soften, dissolve

mend   fix, repair, adjust, regulate   break

merchandise   goods, products, wares

merchant   storekeeper, dealer

merge   combine, unite, mix, blend, join, fuse   separate

merry   gay, happy, lively, jolly, cheerful, jovial   glum

message   word, report, communication, dispatch

messy   sloppy, careless, untidy, dirty   neat

meter   gauge, measure

method   plan, manner, means, system, way, style, procedure

microscopic   tiny, minute   huge

middle   center, heart, core, hub

mighty   strong, powerful, great, grand   weak

mild   gentle, calm, moderate   harsh

military army, troops, soldiers, armed forces

mimic copy, imitate, mock, mime, ape

mind 1. brain, intellect

mind 2. watch, tend, look after

miniature small, tiny, minute giant

minimum least, smallest maximum

minister clergyman, pastor, chaplain

1. minute instant, moment

2. minute tiny, small, miniature giant

miraculous remarkable, wonderful, marvelous, extraordinary, incredible

mischievous naughty, devilish, playful

miserable 1. sad, unhappy, downcast happy

miserable 2. wretched, mean pleasant

misfortune trouble, difficulty, mishap, sorrow

mislead deceive, trick, dupe

misplace lose, mislay

missile rocket, projectile

missing lost, absent, gone present

mission job, errand, task, assignment, chore, duty

mistake error, fault, slip, blunder, oversight

mistreat abuse, molest, manhandle

misty cloudy, foggy, smoky clear

missile

69

misunderstanding difficulty, difference, disagreement

mix blend, combine, join, stir, scramble separate

moan groan, complain, wail

mob crowd, throng, horde

model duplicate, reproduction, likeness, replica

modern new, up-to-date, advanced, contemporary, recent old-fashioned

modest humble, bashful, shy, quiet bold

moist damp, wet, soggy dry

mold 1. shape, form, carve, sculpture

mold 2. decay, rot, spoil

molest harm, mistreat, annoy, abuse

moment instant, minute

monarch ruler, king, sovereign

money currency, cash

monitor helper, assistant

monotonous boring, dull, tedious, humdrum interesting

monster fiend, ogre, demon, freak

mood feeling, temperament, disposition

moody gloomy, glum, depressed, temperamental, sullen

mop scrub, swab

money

70

motion   movement, activity
mountain   hill, elevation
movement   motion, activity
mow   cut, clip, crop, shear
mud   slime, dirt, muck
muggy   humid, damp, sticky, dank
murder   kill, slay, slaughter, execute, assassinate
mutiny   rebellion, revolt, riot, uprising
mystery   puzzle, problem
myth   fable, story, fairy tale, legend

mow

N

nag   pester, annoy, bother
nail   fasten, attach, fix, secure
naked   uncovered, undressed, nude, bare   covered
name   label, tag, title
nap   sleep, doze, drowse, snooze
narcotics   drugs, opiates
narrator   storyteller
narrow   cramped, confined, limited, restricted, close, tight   wide

nap

nasty unpleasant, disgusting, repulsive, offensive, obnoxious pleasant, delightful

nation country, land

natural genuine, real, pure artificial

naturally certainly, surely, of course

naughty bad, disobedient, mischievous good, obedient

near close, at hand far

nearly almost, close to

neat tidy, orderly, well-kept sloppy, messy

necessary needed, important, essential, urgent, required unnecessary

need want, lack, require

neglected overlooked, ignored, slighted protected

neighborhood area, surroundings, vicinity, environment

nerve courage, daring

nervous restless, upset, disturbed, shaken, flustered, tense, edgy, jittery calm

new modern, current, up-to-date, recent old

nice pleasant, agreeable, good, fine unpleasant

noise racket, clamor, commotion, uproar quiet

nominate name, select, choose, designate

nonsense foolishness, stupidity, rubbish, bunk

normal regular, usual, typical, standard, ordinary unusual, abnormal

nosy snoopy, curious, prying

note memo, message

notice see, observe, note

notify tell, report, advise, inform

now immediately, instantly, at once, promptly, presently later

nudge encourage, urge, prod, push, prompt, inspire

nuisance pest, annoyance

numb unfeeling, deadened

number 1. quantity, count, amount

number 2. numeral, figure, symbol, digit

numeral number, figure, symbol, digit

numerous many, a lot, several, various few

nurse care for, tend to, nurture

nutrition food, nourishment

note

O

oath pledge, promise, vow

obey   listen to, mind, comply   disobey

1. object   1. thing, article, item

  object   2. goal, purpose, aim, target

2. object   complain, protest, disagree, challenge, disapprove   approve, agree

obnoxious   nasty, unpleasant, disgusting, hateful, disagreeable, repulsive, offensive   pleasant, agreeable

observe   see, look, watch, study, examine

obstacle   barrier, block, snag, obstruction

obstinate   stubborn, willful, headstrong, pigheaded, ornery   flexible

obstruction   obstacle, barrier, block, snag

obtain   get, receive, gain, acquire

obvious   plain, clear, evident, apparent   vague, unclear

occupation   business, work, job, profession, employment, trade

occur   happen, take place, transpire

odd   strange, unusual, peculiar, queer, weird, bizarre   ordinary

odor   smell, scent, aroma, fragrance

office   1. workplace, studio, headquarters

office   2. position, post, role

often   many times, frequently, repeatedly   seldom

ogre   monster, fiend, demon

old   aged, elderly   young

omit   leave out, miss, skip, exclude   include

only   just, simply, merely

ooze   seep, leak

open   start, begin, launch, establish   close

operate   work, run, manage, handle

opinion   belief, judgment, feeling, sentiment, attitude, view, thought

old

opponent   enemy, competitor, rival, adversary   ally

opportunity   chance, occasion

oppose   fight, disagree, argue, dispute, quarrel, contradict, resist   agree

optimistic   hopeful, cheerful, bright, lighthearted, carefree   pessimistic

oral   spoken, voiced, verbal

orbit   path, circuit, circle, revolution

order   1. arrangement, manner, system

order   2. command, instruction, directive

ordinary   usual, common, normal, average, everyday   unusual

organize   set up, arrange, classify, systematize, categorize

ornament

original 1. firsthand, authentic copied

original 2. novel, new, fresh, different, unique ordinary

ornament decoration, trimming, adornment

ornery 1. stubborn, obstinate, willful, headstrong, pigheaded flexible

ornery 2. mean, cranky, grouchy, cross, difficult pleasant, agreeable

outcome result, effect, end, conclusion, consequence

outfit equip, provide, furnish, supply

outing trip, journey, tour, jaunt, excursion

outline plan, sketch, diagram, draft

outlook view, attitude, position

outrageous absurd, unbelievable, ridiculous, shocking, extreme, ludicrous ordinary, sensible

outstanding important, well-known, great, distinguished, famous, celebrated, prominent ordinary, unimportant

overcast cloudy, dark, dismal clear

overcome conquer, defeat, upset, overpower, surmount surrender, yield

overlook ignore, neglect, disregard, skip, miss

overpass bridge, span, viaduct

oversight error, slip, omission

overthrow defeat, overcome, overpower, destroy, upset

own have, possess

P

pace rate, speed

pack fill, load, stuff empty

pact agreement, understanding, treaty

pad 1. notebook, tablet

pad 2. pillow, cushion

pageant show, exhibition, parade, display, review, spectacle

pad (1)

pail bucket

pain ache, hurt, discomfort, soreness, pang

paint 1. coat, color, cover

paint 2. picture, draw, illustrate, portray, depict

pair set, couple, two

pal friend, companion, buddy, chum

palace castle, mansion, château

pale faint, colorless, wan, pallid bright

pamphlet booklet, brochure, leaflet, folder

palace

77

panic   fear, fright, dread, alarm, terror

pants   trousers, slacks

parade   procession, march, display, review, pageant

parched   dry, thirsty, arid, dehydrated

pardon   forgive, excuse, absolve   blame

part   1. portion, section, segment, piece

part   2. role, character

participate   take part in, partake, contribute, join

particular   fussy, critical, exacting

partner   companion, associate, colleague, collaborator

party   celebration, festivity

party

pass   1. do well, succeed   fail

pass   2. deliver, hand over, transfer

pass   3. throw, toss, fling, hurl, pitch

passage   corridor, lane, opening, channel

paste   glue, mucilage, adhesive

patch   mend, repair, fix

path   route, way, track, trail, lane, road

patience   tolerance, understanding, self-control
   impatience

patriotic   loyal, nationalistic

patrol   watch, guard, protect, police

pattern   1. design, picture, print

path

pattern   2. model, example

78

pause   wait, stop, rest, recess   continue

peaceful   quiet, calm, still, serene   hectic

peak   top, crest, tip, summit   base

peculiar   odd, strange, unusual, queer   ordinary, normal

peddle   sell, vend, hawk

pedestrian   walker

peek   glance, look, glimpse

penalty   punishment, fine

penmanship   handwriting, script

pennant   flag, banner, streamer

pep   energy, spirit, vim, vigor

perfect   faultless, flawless, ideal, excellent   imperfect, defective

perform   do, carry out, achieve, accomplish

perhaps   maybe, possibly, conceivably

period   time, span, interval

perish   die, expire, succumb

permanent   steady, lasting, unchanging, constant   temporary

permit   allow, let, consent

personal   private, individual

perspire   sweat

persuade   win over, convince

peddle

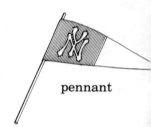

pennant

79

pet (2)

pessimistic   unhappy, hopeless, gloomy, downhearted
optimistic

pester   annoy, bother, disturb, tease, nag, harass

pet   1. favorite, choice

pet   2. stroke, pat, caress, fondle

petite   little, small, slight, tiny   big

petrified   1. scared, frightened, terrified, horrified, shocked, stunned

petrified   2. hardened, stonelike, solidified

petty   unimportant, small, minor, trivial   important

phantom   ghost, spirit, vision, spook, fantasy, illusion

pharmacist   druggist, chemist

photograph   snapshot, picture

physician   doctor, medic

pick   choose, select, elect, opt

picture   illustration, drawing, representation

piece   part, portion, section, segment, bit, chunk, hunk

pier   dock, wharf

pierce   stab, puncture, penetrate

pile   heap, stack, mound, load, collection

pillow   cushion, headrest

pin   fasten, attach, clasp, clip

pioneer   settler, colonist

pistol   gun, revolver, firearm

picture

80

pitch toss, fling, throw, hurl, cast

pity sympathy, compassion

place put, lay, set, deposit, arrange

plain 1. clear, simple, understandable, distinct
complicated

plain 2. unattractive, homely pretty

plan intend, aim, propose

playful frisky, lively, gay, spirited, impish serious

pleasant pleasing, likable, appealing, agreeable,
cheerful, delightful, charming, satisfying
unpleasant

pledge promise, vow, oath, agreement

plenty a lot, sufficient, enough, ample insufficient

plot plan, scheme, concoct

plug block, clog, stop, jam, obstruct open, clear

plump chubby, fat, stout, stocky, heavy, pudgy,
chunky thin

plunge dive, fall, plummet

poetry rhyme, verse

point direct, show, indicate

poisonous toxic, deadly, venomous

poke jab, push, shove, thrust

police guard, watch, protect, defend, shield, secure,
patrol

polish

polish shine, buff, rub, wax, glaze

polite well-mannered, courteous, respectful, gracious rude

poll survey, vote, questionnaire

polluted contaminated, impure, foul, dirty, poisoned clean, pure

poor penniless, needy, impoverished, destitute rich

popular 1. common unusual

popular 2. well-liked, favorite, admired unpopular, disliked

portable movable, mobile, transferable stationary

portion part, section, segment, piece, share

position 1. place, spot, location

position 2. job, role, function

positive sure, certain, definite unsure

possessions belongings, property

possible likely, probable, feasible impossible

post 1. list, notify, announce

post 2. job, position, duty, assignment

postpone put off, delay, stall, procrastinate

pound

pound beat, strike, hit, punch, knock, rap, bang, pummel

power 1. strength, might, force, vigor, energy

power 2. authority, control, influence

82

practically almost, nearly, approximately

practice drill, exercise, train, rehearse

praise compliment, commend, flatter

precious 1. valuable, expensive, costly, priceless
cheap

precious 2. special, loved, adored, cherished

precipitation rain, snow, moisture

precise exact, accurate, definite approximate

predicament mess, dilemma, plight

predict forecast, foresee, prophesy

prefer favor, like, fancy

prejudiced partial, biased fair, neutral

prepare get ready, fix, arrange, concoct

present gift, offering

present

preserve keep, save, hold, maintain, conserve, protect,
guard destroy, neglect

press 1. push, force, squeeze, clasp

press 2. iron, smooth

pretend make believe, act, fake, bluff, feign

pretty attractive, lovely, good-looking homely,
unattractive

prevent stop, block, keep from, deter allow

price cost, value, amount

pride self-respect, self-esteem, dignity

primitive 1. original, ancient, prehistoric   modern

primitive 2. uncivilized, crude, barbaric

principal chief, main, leading

principle rule, law, belief

print publish, issue

prison jail, penitentiary, reformatory

private personal, secret, hidden, intimate   public

privilege advantage, right

prize award, reward, treasure

problem question, issue

procedure plan, practice, rule, policy, way, custom

proceed go ahead, progress, advance

produce make, create, manufacture

profession job, work, occupation, career, vocation

program schedule, plan, list, agenda

progress go ahead, proceed, advance

prohibit forbid, bar, ban, prevent   allow

project undertaking, enterprise, venture

promise agree, swear, pledge, guarantee, vow

promising hopeful, encouraging, favorable

prompt 1. punctual, on time   late

prompt 2. remind, coach, cue

proper correct, right, appropriate, fitting, decent, suitable   wrong, improper

property possessions, holdings, belongings

prosperous successful, comfortable, well-off, rich, wealthy, affluent poor

protect defend, safeguard, shield, support, cover

protest object, complain, challenge

proud pleased, gratified

prove show, demonstrate, document

protest

provide supply, give, furnish

provoke annoy, bother, disturb, tease, taunt, irritate, anger, antagonize

pry 1. meddle, mix, snoop

pry 2. loosen, jimmy

publish print, issue

pull tug, tow, draw, drag, yank, haul push

punch beat, strike, hit, pound, knock, batter, wallop, slug, pummel

pull

punctual prompt, on time late

puncture pierce, stab, penetrate

punish discipline, correct, chastise

pupil student

purchase buy, acquire sell

purify cleanse, clarify, refine, filter soil, pollute

purpose goal, aim, object, target

push press, thrust, shove, force, nudge pull

pupil

85

put   place, lay, set, deposit
puzzle   mystery, problem, enigma

Q

quarrel

quaint   charming, old-fashioned
quake   shake, tremble, vibrate, shudder
qualified   able, capable, fit, competent, suited   unfit
quality   trait, feature, characteristic
quantity   amount, sum, number
quarrel   argue, fight, disagree, differ, dispute, bicker   agree
queer   odd, strange, peculiar, unusual, weird   normal
question   ask, inquire, interrogate   answer
quick   1. fast, rapid, swift, speedy   slow
quick   2. bright, alert, smart, sharp, keen   dull, slow
quiet   silent, still, hushed   noisy
quit   stop, end, cease, halt, conclude, discontinue, finish   continue
quiver   shake, tremble, shiver
quiz   test, examination
quote   repeat, echo, cite

R

race   1. run, speed, rush, dash, hurry, sprint

race   2. nationality, ancestry

racket   1. noise, commotion, uproar, hubbub, din, clamor, disturbance   quiet

racket   2. fraud, swindle

rage   1. anger, violence, frenzy, furor, fit

rage   2. fad, style, fashion

ragged   torn, worn, shabby, tattered, frayed, seedy

raid   attack, invade, assault

raise   1. lift, elevate, boost, hoist   lower

raise   2. produce, rear

rake   collect, gather

rank   grade, class, position

rapid   fast, swift, speedy, quick, hasty   slow

rare   scarce, uncommon, unusual, unique   common

rate   grade, evaluate, rank, appraise

raw   uncooked   cooked

race (1)

ray light, beam, gleam

react respond, answer

ready prepared, set unprepared

real genuine, true, authentic, actual fake

realize understand, grasp, comprehend

rear 1. back, hind front

rear 2. raise, produce

reason explanation, cause, motive, basis, justification

reasonable fair, sensible, just, sound, practical, realistic, rational unreasonable, unfair

rebel disobey, defy, riot, revolt obey

recall remember, recollect, review, reminisce forget

receive take in, get, gain, obtain give

recent new, modern, current, up-to-date, late old

recess pause, stop, rest

recipe instructions, directions, formula

recite tell, relate, narrate, repeat

reckless careless, sloppy, thoughtless, rash, hasty, wild, inconsiderate careful

recognize know, acknowledge

recommend suggest, advise, advocate

record write, list, enter, log

recover 1. get back, regain, rescue, reclaim, retrieve lose

recover 2. get better, improve, heal, rally, recuperate

record

recreation play, amusement, entertainment, pleasure, enjoyment, fun

reduce decrease, lessen, cut increase

referee judge, umpire, mediator

reform improve, change, revise

refrigerate cool, chill

refund repay, reimburse

regal royal, majestic, stately, noble, grand

region district, area, section, location, territory, vicinity, zone

referee

register sign up, enlist, enroll, join

regular common, ordinary, usual, familiar, everyday, typical, normal unusual

rehearse drill, train, practice, repeat, prepare

reject discard, refuse, exclude, eliminate, bar accept

relate tell, recite, narrate, repeat, report, state, recount

related connected, associated, akin

relax rest, unwind

release let go, dismiss, discharge, free hold

reliable dependable, trustworthy unreliable

relief 1. help, assistance, aid

relief 2. ease, alleviation

relief 3. change, substitution, replacement, alternate

relax

89

religious pious, devout

rely depend, count

remain stay, continue

remark statement, comment

remarkable extraordinary, great, special, unusual, exceptional, noteworthy, memorable ordinary

remedy cure, treatment, relief

remember recall, recollect, review, reminisce forget

remove take away, eliminate, discard, withdraw leave

rent lease, let, hire

repair mend, fix, adjust, patch, restore, service break

repeat duplicate, echo

reply answer, response

report tell, recite, narrate, state, describe, recount

request ask for, apply for

require need, lack, want

rescue

rescue save, recover, free, salvage

research exploration, investigation, inquiry, probe

resemblance likeness, similarity

reserve keep, save, hold, put aside

resign give up, leave, quit

respect admire, appreciate, value, honor

respond reply, answer, react

responsible reliable, dependable, trustworthy
  irresponsible

rest 1. pause, relax, unwind

rest 2. remains, balance, leftovers

restless impatient, edgy, uneasy, fidgety calm,
  composed

restore renew, renovate, repair

restriction limitation, restraint

result outcome, end, effect, consequence

retire resign, leave, quit

return 1. go back, revisit

return 2. give back, repay

reunion get-together, gathering, meeting

reveal show, expose, display, disclose hide

review study, remember, recall, learn

revive bring back, resuscitate

revolution 1. revolt, riot, rebellion, uprising

revolution 2. circle, orbit

reward award, payment, prize, compensation

rhythm beat, tempo

rich wealthy, comfortable, well-to-do, affluent, prosperous poor

rip

road

ridiculous foolish, silly, stupid, outrageous, absurd, unbelievable sensible

right correct, accurate, good, fitting, suitable, proper, valid, sound wrong

rigid stiff, firm, unbending, hard soft, flexible

rim edge, border, frame, fringe

riot rebellion, revolt, uprising, brawl

rip tear, cut, split, slit, slash

ripe ready, developed, mature, full-grown green, undeveloped

risk chance, gamble

road path, route, way, thoroughfare

roam wander, drift, meander, ramble, rove

rob steal, loot, burglarize

role part, character

room space, leeway

rot spoil, decay

rotate spin, turn, gyrate, swivel, pivot

rough 1. bumpy, coarse, uneven, jagged, choppy smooth

rough 2. crude, harsh, rowdy, tough gentle

route course, path, rounds

routine habit, system, custom, practice, pattern

rove roam, wander, drift, meander, ramble

row 1. line, series, column, string

row 2. paddle

rowdy rough, disorderly, disobedient, boisterous well-behaved

royal regal, majestic, stately, noble, grand

rubbish waste, garbage, trash, refuse, scrap, junk

rude impolite, disrespectful, discourteous, crude, ill-mannered, curt, insolent polite

rug carpet, mat

ruin spoil, destroy, wreck, demolish, ravage

rule 1. govern, control, regulate, command, manage, head, lead, supervise, direct, run, guide

rule 2. regulation, law

rumor gossip, talk

run 1. race, hurry, hasten, jog, sprint

run 2. govern, control, regulate, command, manage, head, lead, supervise, direct

run 3. operate, work

run 4. flow, stream, pour, gush

run 5. campaign, electioneer

rush hurry, hasten, speed, dash, hustle

rusty corroded

ruthless cruel, mean, heartless, brutal, savage kind

rubbish

S

sacred   religious, holy, spiritual

sad   unhappy, depressed, downhearted, blue, sorrowful, downcast, gloomy, glum, forlorn, dejected, melancholy   happy

safe   secure, protected, guarded   dangerous

sag   droop, hang, drag

salary   pay, wages, compensation

sample   test, try, experiment

sand   scrape, smooth, file, grind

sane   sound, rational, sensible, logical

sanitary   clean, hygienic, sterile   dirty, unsanitary

sarcastic   cutting, bitter, sharp, stinging

satisfied   pleased, content, gratified   displeased

save   1. keep, preserve, conserve, store, accumulate   spend, discard

save   2. rescue, recover, retrieve

say   speak, tell, declare, state, exclaim, express, remark, comment, mention, utter

scald burn, scorch

scar blemish, mark, wound

scarce rare, scanty, sparse plentiful

scare frighten, alarm, startle, shock, unnerve, terrify
calm, soothe

scatter spread, disperse, distribute gather

scene view, sight, setting, picture, vista

scent odor, smell, aroma, fragrance

schedule program, plan, list, agenda, slate, line-up

scheme plot, plan, conspiracy

scold reprimand, chide, admonish

scold

scorch burn, singe, sear, char

score count, sum, tally, total

scoundrel rascal, devil, imp, scamp, villain

scout hunt, seek, search

scramble mix, blend, combine, jumble separate

scrap 1. small amount, shred, speck, fragment

scrap 2. litter, rubbish, junk, trash, garbage, waste,
debris

scrape rub

scratch cut, mark, scrape, scar

scrape

scream yell, howl, cry, shout, screech, wail, shriek

screech shriek, scream, yell, howl, cry, shout, wail,
squeal

seal (3)

screen guard, shield, net

scribble scrawl, scratch

script writing, penmanship

scrub scour, clean, rub, wash

sculpture carve, mold, shape, form, chisel

seal 1. fasten, secure, bind, close, shut open

seal 2. stamp, sign, mark

seal 3. sea lion

sear scorch, burn, singe, char

search scout, hunt, seek

season flavor, spice

secret private, hidden, secluded

section part, portion, segment, piece

secure safe, protected, guarded unsafe, insecure

seek search, scout, hunt

seem appear, look

seep ooze, leak, trickle

segment section, part, portion, piece, division

seize grab, grasp, snatch, clutch release

seldom rarely, hardly, infrequently often

select choose, pick, opt

self-conscious shy, timid, bashful, embarrassed
confident

selfish self-centered, greedy, possessive generous,
good-natured

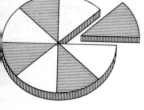

segment

sell peddle, vend buy

send dispatch, forward, transmit receive

sensational marvelous, wonderful, extraordinary, glorious, great, grand, magnificent, splendid, superb, divine, spectacular, exciting, thrilling ordinary, dull

senseless foolish, silly, dumb, stupid, inane sensible

sensible reasonable, logical, practical, realistic, wise, intelligent foolish

separate divide, split, part, sort, isolate join, unite

sequel follow-up, continuation

serious 1. solemn, grave, somber, grim gay, carefree

serious 2. important, major, significant, meaningful unimportant

sermon lecture, talk

serpent snake, viper

serpent

set 1. place, put, lay, deposit, arrange

set 2. fix, adjust, regulate

settle 1. decide, resolve, reconcile

settle 2. locate, occupy, live

several many, numerous, various, some few

severe harsh, cruel, hard, rough, tough, extreme mild

shabby ragged, torn, worn, shoddy, tattered, frayed, seedy

shack

shack hut, cabin, shanty

shake tremble, shudder, shiver, quiver, vibrate

shameful awful, disgraceful, humiliating, scandalous

shampoo soap, lather, wash

shape form, make, develop, fashion, create, construct, mold, design

share divide, split, distribute, apportion

sharp 1. pointy, angular dull

sharp 2. bright, clever, smart, alert, quick-witted, keen, shrewd dull, slow

shatter break, fracture, crack, crush, split, smash, destroy

shelter 1. housing, quarters

shelter 2. protection, cover, refuge

shield protect, defend, safeguard, cover, screen expose

shine glow, gleam, beam, sparkle, glimmer, glisten

shiver shake, tremble, shudder, quiver

shock startle, surprise, stun, jar

shoot fire

shop buy, purchase

shore coast, beach, waterfront

short 1. little, small, puny tall

short 2. brief, concise, succinct long

shampoo

shore

98

shortage lack, want, need, absence, deficiency
abundance

shout scream, yell, howl, cry, call

shove push, bump, nudge

show 1. demonstrate, illustrate, indicate, explain,
clarify

show 2. performance, presentation, production,
exhibit

shrewd sharp, bright, clever, smart, alert, crafty,
quick-witted, keen, sly dull, slow

shriek scream, yell, howl, cry, shout, screech, wail

shrink become smaller, shrivel, wither grow, expand

shudder tremble, shake, shiver, quiver

shuffle mix, scramble, jumble

shut close, fasten, lock, seal open

shy bashful, timid, modest, coy aggressive

sick ill, ailing well, healthy

sight view, scene, vista, picture, spectacle

sign 1. endorse, write, mark

sign 2. signal, motion, gesture, indication

silent quiet, still, hushed noisy

silly foolish, senseless, inane sensible

simple 1. easy, clear, uncomplicated difficult

simple 2. plain, ordinary

sin   evil, crime, offense

sincere   honest, truthful, genuine, unaffected   phony

sing   vocalize, chant

singe   sear, burn, scorch, char

site   place, location, area, spot, region

situation   case, condition, circumstance

skillful   handy, expert, clever, capable, apt, adept   awkward

skimpy   sparse, scanty, scarce   generous

skinny   thin, lean, scrawny, slim   chubby

skip   pass over, leave out, omit, miss, exclude   include

slam   close, bang, shut

slant   slope, tilt, incline

slap   hit, smack, strike

slash   slit, cut, sever, gash

slavery   captivity, bondage   freedom

slay   kill, murder, slaughter, exterminate, destroy

sleep   doze, nap, snooze, slumber

slice   cut, carve, slit

slide   glide, skid, slip

sling   splint, support, bandage

slip   1. slide, skid

slip   2. error, mistake, oversight, blunder

skinny

slide

100

slit   slash, cut, split, gash

slope   slant, incline, tilt

sloppy   careless, messy, untidy, slovenly   neat

slow   1. sluggish, delaying   fast

slow   2. dull, stupid, dim-witted   bright

sly   shrewd, sneaky, crafty, underhanded, shifty

smack   slap, hit, strike, crack, whack, wallop

small   little, slight, puny   big

smart   1. intelligent, bright, alert, wise, clever, quick   stupid

smart   2. pain, ache, hurt

smash   shatter, break, crack, split, destroy, demolish

smash

smear   1. smudge, soil, spot, stain

smear   2. spread, coat, dab

smell   scent, odor, aroma, fragrance

smile   grin, smirk   frown

smog   fog, haziness, cloudiness

smooth   polished, sleek, even   rough

smother   suffocate, muffle, stifle, choke

smudge   smear, soil, spot, stain

snake   serpent, viper

snatch   grab, seize, grasp, clutch   release

snug   cozy, comfortable, secure

soil (2)

soak   wet, drench, saturate   dry

soap   lather, shampoo

sob   cry, weep, bawl

sociable   friendly, cordial   unfriendly

soft   delicate, tender, fluffy, flexible   hard

soggy   damp, wet, moist, watery   dry

soil   1. dirty, spot, stain, smudge, smear

soil   2. ground, earth, dirt

solemn   sad, serious, grave, somber, grim, gloomy, glum   happy

solid   hard, firm, rigid, inflexible, sturdy, strong   soft, flimsy

solution   answer, explanation, finding, outcome, result

solve   answer, explain, figure out

song   tune, melody

soon   shortly, promptly, presently

soothe   calm, comfort, pacify

sore   painful, aching, tender

sorrow   sadness, grief, trouble, misfortune, suffering, misery   joy

sorry   apologetic, remorseful

sort   arrange, organize, classify, group, categorize

sound   noise

souvenir   remembrance, keepsake, memento, token

spacious   roomy, broad, vast   narrow

spar   box, fight

sparkle   shine, flash, glimmer, glitter, glisten, twinkle

speak   talk, comment

special   unusual, exceptional, notable, outstanding, extraordinary, remarkable   ordinary

spectacular   dramatic, sensational, marvelous, wonderful, extraordinary, glorious, great, grand, magnificent, splendid, superb, exciting, thrilling   ordinary, dull

speedy   fast, rapid, swift, quick, hasty

spend   pay out, use   save

spice   season, flavor

spin   turn, twirl, rotate, pivot

spirit   courage, nerve, spunk

spiteful   mean, malicious, vindictive

splendid   glorious, great, grand, magnificent, superb, majestic, wonderful, divine, sensational, marvelous, fine, excellent

split   crack, break, separate, divide

spoil   1. damage, harm, hurt, destroy, ruin, upset, impair

spoil   2. rot, decay

sponsor   backer, supporter, promoter

spin

spot (1)

stage

spook ghost, spirit, phantom

spot 1. soil, dirty, stain, smudge, smear

spot 2. pick out, recognize, identify, spy, sight, distinguish

spread 1. unfold, stretch out, sprawl

spread 2. distribute, scatter, disperse

spry lively, active, energetic, spirited, agile, nimble sluggish

squad group, gang, crew

squander waste, throw away save

squash crush, squeeze, mash

squeeze press, pinch, crush

squirt spurt, splash, spray, spout

stab pierce, puncture, penetrate, perforate

stack pile, heap, mound, load

stage platform, podium

stain dirty, spot, soil, smudge, smear, discolor

stale old, spoiled fresh

stall delay, postpone, procrastinate

stammer stutter, falter

stamp 1. seal, mark, label

stamp 2. pound, bang

stampede rush, panic

stand 1. rise, get up

stand 2. stay, remain, continue

stand 3. suffer, bear, tolerate

stand 4. base, pedestal

stand 5. booth, kiosk

stanza verse, measure

staple attach, fasten, join, connect

star 1. lead, headliner

star 2. heavenly body

stare look, gaze, gape, gawk, glare

start begin, commence, launch end

startle shock, surprise, stun, frighten, upset

starvation hunger, famine

state declare, say, exclaim, announce, tell, express, relate, report

statement account, report, announcement, declaration

station

station stop, depot

stationary fixed, firm, immovable movable

stationery paper, writing materials

statue figure, sculpture

stay remain, continue, stand

steady regular, constant, continuous changing

steal rob, take, burglarize

steam vapor, gas, smoke

statue

105

steer   drive, handle, direct, manage, conduct, lead, head, command, run

step   walk, tread

sterilize   clean, sanitize, disinfect

stern   strict, harsh, rough, tough, hard, severe, firm   lenient, easygoing

stick   attach, adhere, cling

stiff   rigid, firm, unbending, hard, inflexible   flexible

still   quiet, calm, peaceful, serene, tranquil   noisy

sting   prick, wound

stingy   cheap, tight, miserly   generous

stink   smell, odor, stench

stir   mix, blend, combine, scramble

stock   supply, collection, reserve, inventory

stomach   belly, abdomen

stone   rock, pebble

stool

stool   seat, chair

stop   cease, end, halt, quit, conclude, discontinue   start

store   1. keep, stock, collect, save

store   2. shop, market

storm   gale, hurricane, tornado

story   tale, account, narrative

stout   fat, chubby, plump, stocky   thin

strange   odd, unusual, peculiar, queer, weird, bizarre
ordinary

strangle   choke, suffocate, smother

stray   wander, drift, roam, rove, meander

stream   creek, brook

street   road, avenue, thoroughfare

strength   power, force, might, energy, vigor
weakness

stream

stretch   extend, spread, expand

strict   stern, harsh, tough, exact, severe, firm   lenient

strike   hit, bat, slap, smack, slug, swat, knock

strip   remove, uncover, peel, bare   cover

stripe   line, mark, streak

stroke   rub, pet, pat, caress, fondle

strong   mighty, powerful, sturdy, hardy, tough,
healthy, rugged, robust, muscular   weak

struggle   battle, fight, feud, conflict

stubborn   obstinate, willful, headstrong, pigheaded,
ornery   flexible

student   pupil

stuff   fill, load, pack, cram   empty

stumble   trip, tumble, flounder, falter

stun   shock, startle, surprise, daze

stunt   feat, act, performance, exploit

stupid dumb, dull, silly, foolish, dim-witted smart

stutter stammer, falter

stylish fashionable, well-dressed drab

subject topic, issue, theme, question, point, plot

substitute replace, change, exchange, trade, switch

subtract deduct, remove, withdraw add

successful prosperous, well-off, fortunate, winning unsuccessful

sudden unexpected, abrupt, hasty

sufficient enough, plenty, adequate insufficient

suffocate smother, stifle, choke

suggestion proposal, plan, offer

suitable proper, fitting, correct, appropriate improper

sum total, quantity

summary review, outline, accounting

sundown sunset, dusk, evening, nightfall sunrise

sunny bright, cheerful, pleasant dull

sunrise dawn, daybreak, morning sunset

sunset sundown, dusk, evening, nightfall sunrise

superb excellent, fine, splendid, glorious, great, grand, magnificent, wonderful, divine, sensational, marvelous

supernatural ghostly, mystical

supervise   manage, direct, lead, guide, run, control, govern, command, head, boss

supply   provide, give, furnish

support   help, aid, assist, serve, encourage

suppose   believe, think, imagine, consider

sure   certain, positive, definite   uncertain

surplus   extra, additional, spare, leftover, excess   shortage

surprise   astonish, astound, amaze, startle, shock, stun

surrender   give up, quit, yield

surround   encircle, wrap

survive   live, remain, last

suspect   doubt, question, mistrust, distrust   trust

suspense   uncertainty, uneasiness, anxiety

suspension   1. removal, dismissal

suspension   2. interruption, break, pause, intermission

swap   trade, exchange, switch, barter

swat   hit, strike, smack, whack

sway   swing, rock, reel, swagger

swear   1. promise, vow, pledge, guarantee

swear   2. curse

sweep   clean, brush, vacuum

sweet   1. charming, lovely, pleasant, agreeable, adorable   disagreeable

swing

sword

sweet 2. sugary

swift speedy, fast, rapid, quick, hasty slow

swindle cheat, trick, defraud, bamboozle

swing sway, rock, hang, dangle

switch change, exchange, swap, trade, substitute

sword knife, blade

symbol token, emblem

sympathy understanding, pity, compassion

symptom sign, mark, indication

system method, plan, manner, means, way, style, procedure

T

tactful thoughtful, considerate, kind, sensitive, diplomatic tactless

tag 1. follow, shadow, trail, pursue, tail

tag 2. label, name, brand

tail 1. follow, shadow, trail, pursue, tag

tail 2. back, rear, end

take 1. seize, capture, get, obtain give

take 2. carry, bring, transport

tale story, account

talent ability, skill, know-how, gift, forte

talk speak, discuss, converse

tall 1. big, large short

tall 2. high, lofty small

tame gentle, obedient, mild, domesticated wild

tangle twist, knot, snarl

tantrum fit, outburst, flare-up

tap 1. rap, pat

tap 2. faucet, spigot

tap (2)

tape 1. wrap, bind, tie

tape 2. record

target aim, goal, object, purpose

tart sour, sharp, bitter, pungent sweet

task chore, job, work, assignment, duty

taste sample, test, try, savor

tavern inn, bar, saloon, pub

tax duty, toll, tariff

taxi cab, hack

taxi

teach instruct, show, educate, inform, tell, advise, tutor

111

team gang, group, crew, band

tear rip, cut, split, slit, slash

tease annoy, bother, pester, badger, provoke

televise telecast, broadcast

tell relate, recite, narrate, report, state, explain, inform, convey

temperamental moody, sensitive, touchy

temporary passing, momentary, short-lived, transient
permanent

tenant occupant, resident

tense nervous, anxious, strained, uptight, rigid
relaxed

term period, time, duration

terrible horrible, horrid, dreadful, awful, atrocious
wonderful

terrific marvelous, wonderful, glorious, great, magnificent, splendid, superb, sensational ordinary

terrify frighten, scare, alarm, horrify, shock, petrify

territory region, district, area, section, zone

test 1. examine, question, quiz

test 2. try, sample, experiment, attempt

thankful grateful, appreciative

thaw melt, defrost

theater

theater playhouse, hall

thick   broad, bulky, solid   thin

thief   robber, burglar, crook

thin   skinny, lean, slim, slender   fat

think   1. believe, suppose, imagine, expect, guess, suspect, assume

think   2. consider, reflect, ponder

thirsty   dry, parched, dehydrated

thorough   complete, all-out, intensive   incomplete

thought   1. idea, notion, concept

thought   2. care, attention, regard, concern

thoughtful   considerate, kind, sympathetic   thoughtless

thoughtless   inconsiderate, unkind   thoughtful

threaten   warn, bully, intimidate, bulldoze, terrorize, harass

thrifty   economical, careful, frugal   wasteful

thrilling   exciting, delightful, enchanting, stirring, moving, breathtaking   boring

throw   pitch, toss, fling, hurl, cast

throw

ticket   1. pass, voucher

ticket   2. summons, subpoena, citation

tidy   neat, orderly, well-kept, trim   sloppy

tie   fasten, secure, bind, wrap   untie

tight   snug, firm   loose

tilt slope, slant, incline

timid shy, bashful, reserved, meek bold

tint color, dye, stain

tiny little, small, minute, puny huge

tip 1. end, point, extremity

tip 2. gratuity, bonus

tip 3. advice, information, clue

tired exhausted, weary, fatigued rested

title name, heading

toll charge, fee, fare

tone sound, pitch, key

tool instrument, device, implement, utensil, gadget

top head, peak, tip, summit bottom

topic subject, issue, theme, question, point

topple fall, drop, tumble, collapse

torch light, lantern

tornado windstorm, tempest

torture agony, pain, torment

toss throw, pitch, fling, hurl, cast

total 1. whole, entire, complete partial

total 2. add, sum up, count

touch feel, handle, contact

tough 1. hardy, strong, sturdy, rugged, robust weak

torch

tornado

114

tough 2. hard, difficult, rough, complicated easy

tour trip, excursion, journey

tournament contest, game, match, competition

tow pull, haul, drag, tug

toxic poisonous, deadly, venomous

trace copy, reproduce, duplicate, outline

track path, trail, road, course

trade 1. exchange, barter, switch, swap, bargain

trade 2. business, work, line, employment

tradition custom, habit

tragic sad, disastrous, unfortunate, dreadful

trail 1. follow, chase, tail, track, pursue

trail 2. track, path, road, course

train 1. teach, drill, practice, exercise, prepare, condition, groom

train 2. railroad cars

train (2)

traitor betrayer, spy, informer

tramp vagrant, hobo, vagabond

transfer hand over, deliver, pass, change

translate interpret

trap catch, capture, seize, hook, snare release

trash rubbish, waste, garbage, refuse, scrap, junk, litter, debris

travel journey, tour

treasure 1. adore, idolize, cherish, appreciate, value

treasure 2. fortune, wealth, riches

treat 1. deal with, handle, regard, tend to

treat 2. delight, pleasure, thrill

treaty pact, agreement, understanding, alliance

tremble shake, shudder, quiver

tremendous gigantic, colossal, huge, giant, vast, enormous, immense tiny

trial 1. test, experiment, tryout

trial 2. court case

tribe group, clan, sect

trick deceive, mislead, fool, dupe

trim 1. cut, shave, pare

trim 2. decorate, beautify, adorn

trip 1. stumble, tumble, fall, falter

trip 2. tour, journey, excursion

troop group, company, squad, unit

trophy award, prize, reward

trouble bother, difficulty, inconvenience

truant absentee

truce armistice

true genuine, real, pure, authentic, actual, valid, right, proper, correct, accurate, exact false

trust believe, accept distrust

trophy

116

try   test, sample, experiment, attempt

tug   pull, tow, drag, yank, haul

tumble   fall, topple, drop

tune   melody, song

tunnel   passage, channel

turn   rotate, spin, swivel, pivot, twist

tutor   teach, instruct, coach

twinkle   sparkle, shine, glimmer, glitter, glisten, gleam

tumble

twirl   turn, spin, twist, whirl

twist   turn, twirl, spin

twitch   jerk, shudder, spasm

type   kind, sort, variety, class, category, group, species

tyrant   dictator, taskmaster, slave driver

U

umpire

ugly   homely, unattractive, hideous   beautiful

umpire   referee, judge, mediator

unable   unfit, incapable, powerless   able

unanimous   agreed, in accord, harmonious

unaware   ignorant, unknowing   aware

117

unbelievable 1. incredible, absurd, fantastic

unbelievable 2. doubtful, questionable, suspicious
believable

uncertain doubtful, unsure, undecided, unpredictable
certain

unchanged same, steady, constant changed

uncivilized savage, wild, unrefined civilized

uncomfortable awkward, cramped, unpleasant
comfortable

uncommon unusual, rare, scarce, unique, different,
novel, original common

unconscious out cold, senseless, comatose
conscious

unconstitutional unlawful, illegal legal

uncover reveal, show, expose, disclose cover,
conceal

undecided uncertain, doubtful, unsure, indefinite,
vague certain

under below, beneath above, over

understand follow, see, know, appreciate, grasp,
comprehend

undress unclothe, disrobe, strip dress

unemployed jobless, idle, unoccupied employed

unexpected sudden, unforeseen, unplanned
expected

unfair   unjust, partial   fair

unfaithful   untrue, disloyal, fickle   faithful

unfamiliar   strange, unusual, new, different   familiar

unfortunate   unlucky, sad, unhappy   fortunate

unfriendly   antisocial, cool, distant, aloof   friendly

ungrateful   unappreciative, thankless   grateful

unhappy   sad, depressed, dejected, downhearted, blue, sorrowful, downcast, gloomy, glum, forlorn, melancholy   happy

unhappy

unhealthy   sickly, ill, ailing, frail, weak   healthy

uniform   outfit, costume

unimportant   petty, minor, trivial, insignificant   important

unnecessary   needless, useless, uncalled-for   necessary

unoccupied   vacant, available, open, empty   occupied

unpack   unload, empty   pack

unpleasant   nasty, disagreeable, unlikable, offensive, obnoxious   pleasant

unpopular   disliked, unwanted   popular

unreasonable   ridiculous, absurd, extreme   reasonable

unruly   disorderly, wild, disobedient   orderly

unsafe   dangerous, risky, hazardous   safe

unsatisfactory   poor, inferior, second-rate, inadequate
satisfactory

unsuccessful   failing, unfortunate   successful

untie   loosen, undo, unfasten   tie

unusual   uncommon, rare, unique, different, novel,
original   usual

unwilling   opposed, reluctant   willing

uphold   support, maintain, defend, back

upright   1. standing, erect, vertical

upright   2. honorable, respectable, moral

uprising   revolution, revolt, riot, rebellion

uproar   noise, racket, clamor, commotion, disturbance,
tumult, hubbub   peace

upset   disturb, annoy, bother, unnerve   soothe

urge   push, press, advise, prod, coax, prompt
discourage

urgent   necessary, important, essential, vital, crucial
unimportant

useful   helpful, practical, handy, valuable, beneficial
useless

useless   worthless   useful

usher   guide, escort

usual   common, regular, normal, ordinary, familiar,
everyday, typical   unusual

usher

120

V

vacant unoccupied, available, open, empty filled, occupied

vacation leave, break, recess, holiday

valuable important, significant, precious, costly, expensive

value worth, cost

vandalism destruction, ruination

vanish disappear, fade appear

vapor steam, fog, mist

various several, different, many, numerous, assorted

vary change, alter

vast huge, immense, enormous, great tiny

vegetation plants, growth, flora

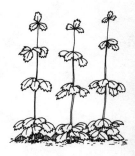

vegetation

verdict decision, ruling, finding, judgment

verse 1. poetry, rhyme

verse 2. passage, section, part, division

version account, story, description, interpretation

veto refuse, deny approve

vibrate   shake, quiver

vicious   ferocious, fierce, savage, brutal, cruel, ruthless, evil, wicked, mean

victim   loser, underdog, sufferer, prey

victory   triumph, success, winning   defeat

view   sight, scene, vista, picture

villain   scoundrel, rascal, devil

violate   break, disobey

violence   rage, anger, frenzy, fury

vision   1. eyesight, perception

vision   2. image, illusion, fantasy, dream

volunteer   offer, come forward

vote   ballot, choice, selection

voyage   journey, cruise, crossing

W

wake

wag   wave, flap, swing, shake

wake   get up, arise

walk   stroll

wallop   smack, slap, hit, strike, crack, whack, thrash, beat, slug

wander   stray, drift, roam, rove, ramble

want   desire, wish for, long for, crave

war   battle, fight, feud, struggle, combat, conflict

warn   1. caution, inform, notify, alert

warn   2. threaten

wash   launder, clean, scrub

waste   squander, misuse   save

wash

watch   1. observe, see, look at

watch   2. guard, protect, defend, shield

wave   sway, move, flap

wax   polish, shine, glaze

weak   feeble, frail, powerless   strong

wealthy   rich, comfortable, well-to-do, affluent, prosperous   poor

wed   marry, join, unite

weird   queer, odd, strange, peculiar, unusual, creepy, spooky, eerie   normal

welcome   greet, receive

wed

whack   wallop, smack, slap, hit, strike, crack, thrash, beat, slug

whip   strike, beat, thrash, flog, crack

whole   complete, total, entire   partial

wicked   evil, bad, sinful, mean, cruel, ruthless, vicious   good, saintly

wide   broad, expansive   narrow

win

wife   spouse, mate, married woman

wig   hairpiece

wild   1. untamed, uncivilized, savage, ferocious
civilized, tame

wild   2. reckless, rash, crazy, frenzied   calm

willing   agreeable, ready, consenting   unwilling

win   succeed, triumph, prevail   lose

1. wind   air, breeze, gust

2. wind   turn, twist, coil

wire   telegraph, cable

wise   smart, intelligent, clever, knowledgeable,
learned, educated, scholarly   uneducated

wish   desire, long for, want, crave

withdraw   remove, subtract, deduct   deposit

without   lacking, wanting, needing, missing, minus,
less   with

witty   clever, amusing, funny, humorous

wonderful   marvelous, glorious, great, grand, magnificent, splendid, superb, divine, sensational, spectacular   horrible

woods   forest

work   1. labor, toil

work   2. operate, run, manage, handle

workout   exercise, practice, drill

world   universe, earth

worn   used, old, secondhand, ragged   new

worried   troubled, concerned, disturbed, upset,
nervous   calm

worship   adore, idolize, cherish, revere

wound   injury, hurt, bruise

wrap   cover, bind, tie   uncover

wreath   garland

wreck   destroy, ruin, demolish

wring   squeeze, twist

wrong   incorrect, inaccurate, faulty, mistaken   right

wreath

X

x-ray   picture, photograph

Y

yacht   boat

yacht

125

yarn

yank pull, tug, jerk

yarn wool, thread

yell shout, scream, howl, cry, call, shriek, screech

yield 1. produce, give, provide, supply

yield 2. surrender, give up, sacrifice

young youthful, juvenile old

youngster child, minor, youth, kid

Z

zero nothing, nil, none

zone region, district, area, section, territory

zoo menagerie

zoom speed, zip, whiz, fly